Dr. Potts, My Pets Have SPOTS!

To the memory
of Rod Hull

To all of the lovely
and helpful staff at
Mullacott Veterinary
Hospital — M. L.

First published in Great Britain
by Barefoot Books, Ltd
and in the United States of America
by Barefoot Books, Inc in 2017
All rights reserved

Barefoot Books, 2067 Massachusetts Ave
Cambridge, MA 02140

Barefoot Books, 29/30 Fitzroy Square
London, W1T 6LQ

Text copyright © 2000 by Rod Hull
Illustrations copyright © 2017 by Miriam Latimer
The moral rights of Rod Hull and Miriam Latimer
have been asserted

Graphic design by Judy Linard,
Design for Publishing, London and
Sarah Soldano, Barefoot Books

Reproduction by Bright Arts, Hong Kong

Printed in China on 100% acid-free paper

This book was typeset in Jolly Good Proper,
Campland Letters, Olivier, Bluberry Regular
and HipHop

The illustrations were prepared in acrylics
and collage

HB ISBN: 978-1-78285-319-0
PB ISBN: 978-1-78285-324-4

British Cataloguing-in-Publication Data:
a catalogue record for this book is
available from the British Library

Library of Congress
Cataloging-in-Publication Data
is available upon request

1 3 5 7 9 8 6 4 2

Dr. Potts, My Pets Have SPOTS!

Written by
Rod Hull

Illustrated by
Miriam Latimer

Barefoot Books
step inside a story

Mr. Betts, who had lots of pets,
Went in a panic, one day, to the vet's.

The vet, whose name was Dr. Potts,
Listened and said, "You *have* got lots
    and lots of pets.
What's wrong with them, Mr. Betts?"

Poor Betts sighed, "Oh Dr. Potts!
My pets have all got lots of spots:

A spotty fish, a spotty cat,
a spotty snake, a spotty rat,
A spotty rabbit, a spotty frog,
a spotty canary, a spotty dog."

"Dear me, dear me," said Dr. Potts,
And searched through her book
'til she came to "spots."

"Now, strawberries suffer from botrytis.
It seems your pets have ... spottyitis."

"Spottyitis? Is that bad?"
(Poor Mr. Betts was feeling sad.)

"Nothing bad that
    I can't cure!"
(Though Dr. Potts
    was not quite sure.)
She thought of pills
    or, perhaps, a lotion,
But decided on
    a special potion.

She mixed it up
    behind a screen
And returned with
    a medicine that was
        bright GREEN.

"Give them this
    three times a day.
That should take
    the spots away."

et better.

The spots went away!
(Which was a surprise.)
But Mr. Betts couldn't believe his eyes.
He looked at his pets and shouted,
"YIKES!"

No more spots . . . they were covered in STRIPES!

Off at once, back to the vet's,
Ran an angry Mr. Betts.

"Stripes?" said a startled Dr. Potts.
"You mean they've got stripes
    instead of spots?"

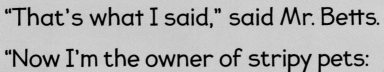
"That's what I said," said Mr. Betts.
"Now I'm the owner of stripy pets:

A stripy fish, a stripy cat,
a stripy snake, a stripy rat,
A stripy rabbit, a stripy frog,
a stripy canary, a stripy dog."

It was obvious something
had gone wrong.
Perhaps the green stuff
was much too strong.

"Aha!" said the vet.
"I know what to do.

Green's no good.
Give them this...it's BLUE."

With the blue medicine,
    Mr. Betts went away,

But you'll never
    guess what…
he was back
    the next day.

"Hello!" Dr. Potts said. "Did that do the trick?
Tell me your pets are no longer sick."

"Well," began Betts, as he faced Dr. Potts,
"The green stuff you gave me got rid of the spots,
But gave them a bad case of stripes instead,
So I gave them the blue stuff, just like you said.
The stripes went away but it's worse than I feared...
Now each of my pets has grown a BEARD!

A bearded fish, a bearded cat,
a bearded snake, a bearded rat,
A bearded rabbit, a bearded frog,
a bearded canary, a bearded dog. ,,

"Aha! That's easy to cure, my good fellow.

Give them this twice a day...it's YELLOW!"

So once again, Mr. Betts

went away.

And once again he was back the next day.
"The green stuff you gave me," he said, "Dr. Potts,
Was quite successful — it got rid of the spots,
But gave them a bad case of stripes instead,
So I gave them the blue stuff just as you said.
Then, as you saw, the stripes disappeared
But left all my pets with very long beards.

So I gave them the yellow stuff and by and by,
the beards went away...
but they started to CRY!

A crying fish, a crying cat,
A sobbing snake, a sobbing rat,
A weeping rabbit, a weeping frog,
a wailing canary, a wailing dog."

And chose a medicine that was...

bright RED!

Poor Mr. Betts, he gave a sigh.

Anything was worth a try.

Taking the medicine, he ran from the vet's.

But back the next day came Mr. Betts.

Dr. Potts was getting vexed

And wondering what would happen next.

Mr. Betts looked a sorry sight,
As if he had been up all night.

"Did it work, Mr. Betts?" the vet inquired.

"Did it give you the results that you desired?"

"Well the green stuff you gave me, Dr. Potts,

Worked a treat — no more spots.

But as you know, they got stripes instead,

So I gave them the blue stuff,

　　like you said.

No more stripes, but rather weird,

All my pets grew a very long beard.

So I gave them the yellow stuff to try

And all my pets began to cry.

Next was the red stuff and — no surprise —

They stopped crying at once ...

...but they've SHRUNK IN SIZE!

A very small fish, a very small cat,
A little snake, a little rat,
A minute rabbit, a minute frog,
a tiny canary, a tiny dog."

"Then we've won, Mr. Betts!
   Oh, how splendid.
We'll start from scratch —
   your troubles have ended.
Your pets are precious,
   I know you need them.
Now all you have to do
   is feed them!"

A whole week passed

And then at last

Hurrying, scurrying into the vet's

Came a delighted Mr. Betts.

Gone were the spots, the stripes, and the beards,
Gone were the weeping and wailing and tears.
Grinning and beaming, Mr. Betts
Was proud to show off his HEALTHY pets!

Happy now, he rides the streets
And tells each passerby that he meets,
"I've got...

A healthy fish, a healthy cat,
    a healthy snake, a healthy rat,
A healthy rabbit, a healthy frog,
    a healthy canary, a healthy dog."